I0703997

Spook

my best friend

by

Alexander Francis

Spook

my best friend

Copyright ©2023 by Alexander Francis
Arcus Verba Publishing
P.O Box 210
De Forest, Wisconsin
53532
www.arcusverba.com

TM

Cover design by Alexander Francis
Graphic images by Alexander Francis

ISBN: 978-1-942420-28-6 print edition
ISBN: 978-1-942420-29-3 e-book

Novels by Alexander Francis

Revenge of Jesus

Are We A Band Yet

Mick Grundy...Spy Hunt

Mick Grundy...The Russian Connection

Mick Grundy...Elapid

Geminknot

Beware The Exit

The Green Scarf

Memory Gap

The Copy Candidate

Since Antonius

Please visit afnovels.com for more information

Spook   *by Alexander Francis*

Foreward

This book was written for the entertainment of children who have had experiences with a beloved family dog, or yearn for one. It is a brief but intense story of love and affection which can happen between a young master and their family dog. And, as inevitably occurs, there is separation, grief, followed by maturity which develops after final parting, leaving the young adult with enduring memories but an aching heart along with a better understanding of life and its purpose.

Thanks to my assistants, proofreaders and consultants for their assistance in writing this book.

And a special thanks to Kira and her dog Casper for posing for photography....and for her wonderful narration as well as her sitting for the videos. I could not and would not have attempted this without Kira.

Alexander Francis

Table of Contents

Chapter One...The Beginning

Luna is ten years old and is having a birthday celebration. She is seated at the head of the table with a small cake in front of her, lit with ten burning candles.

"Do you have any wishes to make before you blow out the candles?" asked her father while gently patting her arm. Luna nodded 'yes' and looked around at her parents before puffing out a big breath of air which extinguished the candles. This was followed by a stream of smoke slowly rising in the air above the cake.

Her mother clapped and started organizing the plates for the slices of cake about to be cut. "What did you wish for?" she asked.

Luna cast her eyes downward toward the cake. "Same thing. I don't want to talk about it."

"I know what you wished for," her father admitted while smiling broadly. "We think it's about time you get your wish," he said, nodding and looking kindly at her.

Luna stared at him intently, scanning his face, searching for the meaning of his statement. She watched as he rose from his chair and left the room. Somewhere in the distance, she heard the back screen door shut. Luna gave her mother a quizzical look.

"He will be right back, my dear," her mother assured her. In a moment or two, she heard the squeak of the old screen door and her father talking softly to someone as his footsteps grew closer.

Luna focused on the doorway, anticipating her father accompanied by an unknown guest. Could it be that her sister Ann has returned from college to be with her on her birthday? A movement caught her eye as a white object started slowly to emerge from behind the door frame. White was followed by black and the face of a puppy slid into view. He had black eyes, a red nose and his neck was extended as he tried to look around the room from his perch in her father's arms.

"A puppy!" Luna sputtered while coming to her feet. She rushed over, extending her hand to caress this wonderful gift, this white puppy, her wish come true at last. She looked up at her father's grin then back to the puppy who was making an attempt to lick her hand.

"What kind of dog is this, Father, and what is his name?" she squealed.

Her father put the puppy down on the floor, and they all laughed as he wagged his tail so hard that his entire rear half was also wagging. Luna started petting him with both hands, and the puppy used his mouth and tongue to wrap around her arm or hand or any part of her he could touch.

"This is a Lab," he answered "and he has no name as yet. You can decide on a name when you're ready."

"Oh, I already know his name," Luna answered, glancing up. "This is Spook. Spook, meet my dad." Luna pushed the puppy, now being called Spook, toward her father's legs, and his hand came down to also pet this very energetic puppy.

Mother spoke up, "Luna, you are to be responsible for Spook from now on. You have to train him to be housebroken, and you have to train him to take commands before he will become a good pet. We are going to teach you how to do all that."

"Can Spook sleep with me?" Luna asked, looking back and forth with pleading in her eyes.

"Eventually," Father answered. "First, he has to be housebroken and has to sleep in his cage until the training is over. "And," he continued, "after that, he will have a bed on the floor in your room, if you like."

Luna blinked, taking in what her father had said. She suddenly had the start of tears in her eyes, and she stood up looking back and forth at her parents. "You mean, Spook can't sleep with me?" she asked.

"Not in your bed," Mother answered. "Spook will be a very big dog in a few months and, trust me, both of you will be better off if he sleeps on the floor on his own bed."

Luna nodded that she understood though she still had doubts that it was the best way. She had been waiting on a dog she could call her own for months, years even, and at last it was true. Spook was hers and hers alone. Such joy! She squatted down again and extended her arms, and Spook ran into her so fast that it nearly knocked her to the floor. She had to extend her neck and turn her face away from him so that she could stay clear of his long wet tongue.

   Luna placed her hands on either side of Spook's face and held his eyes with hers. "Spook, my Spook, you are mine now, and we are going to look after each other. Isn't that so?"

Spook writhed around and licked her arm broadly before looking back at her face. His eyes answered. He was hers, and she was his from this day forward and forever.

Chapter Two...Bonding

As the days and weeks came and went, Luna and Spook followed each other almost as if Spook had become her shadow. When she sat down, Spook sat near her feet, often on top of her feet. He would look longingly at her face and give her ankles an appropriate lick from time to time. When Luna went to the bathroom and closed the door, Spook stationed himself on the outside and no matter how long it took for Luna to come out, Spook was there to greet her as if they had been parted for years instead of minutes.

Spook gained size and weight rapidly, nearly matching Luna for size in just two months. He was inquisitive about everything, inspecting, sniffing and licking any object or person close enough. It was as if Spook was learning about the world through his nose and tongue. When there was a lull in activity, Spook chose to carry something up the long flight of stairs, drop it on the first step, watch it tumble into the downstairs hall and then slide down the same stairs on his tummy. The family often watched with humor, laughing out loud and then laughing again as Spook stopped, cocked his head and wondered what the fuss was all about.

   Luna could tell that Spook was smart because he learned quickly what was expected of him. All it took was a low spoken command, especially from Luna, and Spook would stop what he was doing and immediately obey. At night, and as Luna wanted, Spook would accompany her to her room and carelessly plop himself down on his bed beside hers. He would exhale noisily, more like a big audible sigh, expressing some displeasure on not being able to jump into bed with Luna. If he needed to go outside during the night, he would rest his head on her bed in clear view of Luna's face and moan softly. When this didn't work soon enough for him, licking would. Luna would awaken enough to see him close by and sleepily understand that he needed her help. At times she was suspicious that all Spook really wanted was to go explore in the middle of the night, accompanied by Luna.

   As the months went by, the bond between Luna and Spook grew stronger and more mature. Each morning, Luna, as she left for school, would instruct Spook to 'sit' before she left by the front door. Spook would sit in the same spot, his big dark eyes on her as she slipped on her coat and hat. The last thing she would do is to bend down and stroke Spook's neck while whispering, "Be good, Spook, and I'll see you this afternoon." Then she would open the door and step across the threshold with one last, over her shoulder, look at Spook, who remained motionless. His big sorrowful eyes beamed regret to her, but he stayed in place until the door fully closed. Afterwards, he would dart to the windows, running back and forth as he sought to have the last look of his departing Luna.

In the afternoons, Spook always seemed to know the exact moment Luna would arrive, and he was sure to be in his spot, seated but intent, a broad smile on his face. Nor would he change position until she was fully in the house, and she greeted him with her usual, "Hi Spook! Are you glad to see me?" Certainly he was glad, and he would explode with energy, standing on his rear feet and putting his paws on her shoulders, seeing her eye to eye, his wonderful Luna.

Luna always made time in the afternoons to take Spook for a walk or to just play run and catch the ball. Spook never seemed to tire and was deliriously happy just to be with his Luna. The two were inseparable once again until Luna left the next morning.

Chapter Three...Lost

One day, Luna got off the bus near her home and started up the small hill. It had been a very fine day. Her grades were very good, the sky was clear and warm, and her friends had been fun to be with. She had not thought about her best friend all day but now she looked forward to opening the door and seeing him in his spot, trembling with excitement that she was home.

Luna smiled in anticipation as she opened the door. The spot where Spook always sat was empty. Where was Spook? Was he hiding from her or with her mother? Luna's face fell a little bit as she began to be disturbed by this change in the expected. For three years, every day had been the same: She would open the door and see Spook sitting in his spot, his pink tongue visible, and the corners of his mouth pulled back into a familiar smile. She would greet him in the usual way, and he would bolt forward to wrap himself around her, wagging his tail as fast as he could. Then he would stand up and look into her face with his happy eyes.

"Mother!" she called out while putting her backpack on the floor. "Mother!" she called again, louder this time. In the distance, she heard a faint reply, and she hurried to the laundry room expecting to see both her mother and Spook.

Luna pushed open the door, looking around, as she came into the small room. Her mother stood up from the clothes basket and smiled as she pushed a strand of hair back into place. "Did you have a good day in school?" she asked.

"I did, Mother. And are you having one also?" Luna responded.

"I guess. Just trying to catch up with some housework. Do you care for a snack?" her mother asked.

"Where is Spook?"

"I haven't paid attention. I've been so busy. Isn't he there with you?" her mother asked, trying to look past Luna for the familiar big white head. "In fact, now that I think about it, I don't remember seeing him since early this morning."

"I'll find him," Luna assured her. She turned and started clapping and calling out, "Spook! Here Spook!" She ran upstairs to look in Spook's bed, then cast her eyes around the hall, running to each room in return with the same result. Spook was not there. Panic started to creep into Luna's mind. Where was Spook? He had to be here.

"Did you find him?" her mother called from downstairs.

"Not yet" she answered. "We should look in all the rooms and even in the garage." Luna said loudly, her voice rising in pitch a bit.

Together they did a complete search of the house and even their yard. Spook clearly wasn't there. Yelling his name outside had the same result. Spook was gone.

They stood together on the sidewalk outside their home, both looking in different directions, hoping in their minds that they would soon see the big white dog streaking toward them. But wishes are not the same as real life. Spook was nowhere in sight.

"Mother?" Luna said, "Do you see any way Spook could have left the house?"

"I did find the front door partially opened this morning after you left. I just assumed that you didn't close it fully."

"No, I remember closing the door. You know, I have seen Spook playing around with the handle. He is very smart, and I'll bet he figured out how to open the door. That explains it. Spook went out looking for me." Luna started forming tears that ran slowly down her cheeks. That was the answer: Spook has been wandering around, far from home, trying to find her. The truth came as a flash to her mind. Spook was probably lost but still looking for her.

Chapter Four...The Search

It was a long afternoon. Luna and her mother searched the neighborhood, called their friends, knocked on all the doors in the neighborhood...and not a trace of Spook could be found. No one had seen him. They felt lost. Finally, later in the afternoon, Father came home and was quickly involved in their dilemma. He suggested that they start driving down all the streets close to home and then extend the search as far as Luna's school.

It seemed more and more hopeless as the hours went by and the sky started to darken with evening approaching. Father called the Police and all the veterinarian offices as well as the Animal Control office. No one had even heard of a big white dog being either lost or found. Where was Spook?

During and after supper there was near silence. Nobody had any more ideas of what to do or where to look. Not having Spook nearby as they ate was unsettling. Without realizing it, each of them would occasionally look around, expecting to see that big white dog looking back, probably wondering how their food tasted and when was he going to be allowed to try out some. Their memory could see him licking his lips, sending a message that he wanted some also. After all, in Spook's mind, he was one of them, an equal part of the family.

At bedtime, Luna entered her room, giving it a complete visual search just in case they had all missed old Spook somehow. But he wasn't there...his bed was imprinted with his body, and in Luna's imagination, Spook was somehow looking back at her waiting patiently for his goodnight caress. More than ever, Luna realized that Spook was more than a pet, he was her companion that she could always talk to, always ruffle his fur absentmindedly, and always count on to warn or defend her, no matter what.

It was hard to sleep not knowing where Spook was sleeping or if he was safe and uninjured. But when sleep finally came, he came back to her in her dreams. The big harmless goofball of a dog who had boundless energy and endless love in his heart. Spook had learned all the commands that Luna knew could be given, and more. Big old Spook seemed to have extraordinary perception of her moods, not approaching her when she was angry or tense but pressing against her and licking her anywhere when she was sad or hurt.

Luna awakened with the coming dawn, fully expecting the big white head to be resting near her pillow, waiting patiently for her to look his way. But then she remembered...Spook wasn't there, and there was an increasing chance that he would never be there again. She sat up and looked at the wall while she thought it out. They had to run a search using the Net and the paper, a missing dog report. And she also recalled that Spook was not wearing his collar the day he went missing. She had taken it off because it was irritating his neck. He had no identifying tags, so if he were found, there was no way of knowing where he belonged. Luna put her hands to her face and wept abundant tears. It was her fault Spook was gone, and there was no undoing it.

 Spook

Chapter Five...Spook Comes Home

It happened just after breakfast and before Luna left for school. A quiet tap on the front door, almost too soft to notice at first. Luna opened the door to find an older and stooped woman looking back with faded eyes.

"Are you the owner of a big white dog?" the lady asked.

Luna was nearly too stunned to answer and at first looked past the woman in search of Spook. All she saw was a large dark car parked at the curb.

"We have a big white Lab named Spook who just went missing. Yes, I am his owner." Luna answered. "Do you know where he is?"

"Sure do," the woman answered. "Say, what is your name?" she asked.

"I am Luna," she answered

"Well, Luna, you can come out to the car and see if this one is yours. We found him yesterday evening and didnt see any tags. We took him over to the Vet this morning and had him read the chip. They gave us this address." With that, the lady turned her back and started moving toward the waiting car. Luna followed.

The back door was opened and before Luna could clearly see the inside, a loud bark came roaring out. Then she saw his face. No doubt in the world. This dog was Spook, and he was panting and pulling at his leash toward her.

"That's my dog." Luna squealed in delight, and leaned into the car to touch him, trying to avoid his big tongue.

"Well, he's yours. You can take him. Too big for us anyway, and I can tell you, he eats like a horse. However can you afford to keep him?" the lady stated.

Once unclipped, Spook came rushing out of the car, streaking up and down through the yard, his eyes centered at all times on the one he loved the most and who was standing there with a big smile on her face watching his antics.

"Oh, and you don't need to thank us. I lost a dog once, and I know how it feels. Better keep track of this one so it can't happen again." the lady said and finally smiled at her. She closed the door of her car, and it drove silently off.

Luna gave a single clap, and as if by magic, Spook appeared at her right side, seated himself and looked up at her with all the love he could muster. They were again united and there for each other for as long as life continued.

 Spook

Addendum

The day had finally come...the last day, the last moment, before she left for college. Luna knew that someday this moment would arrive, where time seems to stop and then start over with new goals, new friends and new situations. Luna had grown up, and the happy childhood she recalled so vividly was done and over, and she was stepping into a new world starting right now.

Spook was sitting down just in front of her, his big dark eyes a mystery to what he was thinking. He seemed to know that this was an important moment, but he had dignity and strength and would endure what he had to endure. There was so much to say to this big white dog, so many memories that he was part of, but there were no words to express the love Luna had for him and the sorrow that she felt in parting from him. She knew that dogs have a shorter life span than humans, and Spook's life was not too far from the end. It was possible that she would never see his face again, never feel his warmth, his wonderful fur or his patient stare. There was no way to stop time or go back to her youth and its adventures. Life has a progression, and this was one moment of it. She felt warm tears start down her face, and she was sure that Spook could see them also but he stayed seated and just looked at her as she looked at him, trying to burn these last images into memory. This was goodby, probably for eternity.

Luna waved goodby to Mother and Spook as the car started slowly moving away, and her mother waved back. Luna continued to look backward as the pair got smaller and smaller and finally were gone.

The End